Bob and the Pink Wig

Written by Zoë Clarke

Illustrated by Susan Batori

Collins

Bob has a pink wig ...

2

and pink dogs.

Gulls tug the wig.

5

Bob runs up the long hill.

6

The gulls hang the wig ...

on a van.

Bob thinks.

11

Bob winks.

Bob has a pink wig!

13

/w/

14

After reading

Letters and Sounds: Phase 3

Word count: 40

Focus phonemes: /v/ /w/ /th/ /ng/ /nk/

Common exception words: the, no, my, you

Curriculum links: Understanding the World: People and communities

Early learning goals: Understanding: answer "how" and "why" questions about their experiences and in response to stories or events; Reading: children use phonic knowledge to decode regular words and read them aloud accurately, read some common irregular words, demonstrate understanding when talking with others about what they have read

Developing fluency

- Your child may enjoy hearing you read the book.
- As you read, ask your child to play the part of Bob by reading the speech bubbles on pages 5, 7 and 11 with lots of expression. You may wish to model reading one of them first.

Phonic practice

- Look at the inside front cover and point to the grapheme "ng". Say the sound together.
- Now look at page 6 together. Ask your child if they can spot a word that contains "ng". (*long*)
- Turn to page 8 and ask your child to find a word that contains the letters "ng". (*hang*)
- Look at the "I spy sounds" pages (14–15). Say the sounds together. How many items can your child spot that contain the /v/ sound in them? (*vet, van, violin*) Can they find any items with the /w/ sound in them? (*water, walk, wave, watch*)

Extending vocabulary

- Go through the book again and ask your child to think of new speech bubbles for Bob. What else might he say on pages 5, 7 and 11?